The Case of the
DOUBLE
CROSS

An I Can Read Book®

The Case of the
DOUBLE
CROSS

written and illustrated by
Crosby Bonsall

A Harper Trophy Book

Harper & Row, Publishers

I Can Read Book is a registered trademark
of Harper & Row, Publishers, Inc.
The Case of the Double Cross
Copyright © 1980 by Crosby Bonsall
For information address Harper & Row, Publishers, Inc.,
10 East 53rd Street, New York, N.Y. 10022. Published simultaneously
in Canada by Fitzhenry & Whiteside Limited, Toronto.
Library of Congress Catalog Card Number: 80-7768
ISBN 0-06-444029-X
First Harper Trophy edition, 1982.

"Mean, mean, full of beans,

hope you get a hole in your jeans!"

"Mean, mean, full of beans,

hope you get a hole in your jeans!"

"It's old Marigold,"

Snitch told his brother Wizard

and their friends Skinny and Tubby.

9

The boys were private eyes.

They had their own clubhouse.

The sign on the door said:

NO GIRLS.

Wizard, the chief private eye,

put it up a long time ago.

Marigold and Gussie and Rosie

hated that sign.

Each day Marigold shouted,

"Mean, mean, full of beans,

hope you get a hole in your jeans!"

Each night she dreamed of ways

to join the club.

Marigold dreamed

she had a horse.

She let

the boys

ride it.

They begged her

to join their club.

Marigold dreamed

she saved the boys

from a terrible flood.

They begged her to join their club.

15

Marigold dreamed

she ran an ice-cream stand.

Marigold gave the boys

all the ice cream they could eat.

They begged her to join their club.

17

But THEY DIDN'T!

Marigold called Rosie and Gussie.

"I have a plan,"

she told them.

Next morning, a funny little man

with a long, long beard

handed Snitch a letter.

"For you and Wizard,

and Skinny and Tubby,"

mumbled the funny little man.

And he ran away.

"I can't read it," Wizard shouted.

"It's in code," Skinny said.

"Who gave it to you?" asked Tubby.

"A funny little man

with a long, long beard," Snitch said.

"We have to find him!" Wizard said.

"Let's go, men."

They looked everywhere.

But they did not find

the funny little man.

23

"Fine private eyes we are,"

Wizard groaned.

"Hey, there he is!" Snitch cried.

"Follow him!" Wizard shouted.

The funny little man

with the long, long beard

ran fast.

The boys ran after him.

Wizard passed him.

Snitch bumped into him.

26

Tubby almost grabbed him.

Skinny tripped over him.

27

"He ran away from me," Snitch wailed.

"We have to catch him," Skinny said,

"and make him tell us the code."

"Mean, mean, full of beans,

hope you get a hole in your jeans!"

"Marigold can help us catch him,"

Snitch told his brother.

Wizard scowled. "Get lost!

What do girls know?"

29

"What are you doing?" Marigold asked.

"Get lost," Wizard snapped.

"If I get lost, you'll be sorry,"

Marigold warned him.

"You heard me," Wizard growled.

"Here's the case,"

Wizard told the private eyes.

"We have a funny little man.

We have a letter in code.

We can't break the code.

We can't even find the man!"

"And there are four of us,

and only one of him." Tubby sighed.

"But he knows us," Snitch said.

"He gave the letter to me

and he knew our names."

"He's out to get us," Tubby cried.

Wizard scowled.

"We're looking for HIM," he shouted.

Snitch remembered something.

"But he found ME!"

"That's right," Wizard cried,

"we will let him find US.

We will set a trap!"

Snitch stood by the tree

where the funny little man

had given him the letter.

Tubby and Skinny and Wizard

hid behind the tree and waited.

At last they heard footsteps.

It was the funny little man.

The boys grabbed him.

"Yeow!"

yelled the funny little man.
"Get off my thumb!"
yelled the funny little man.
"HELP! HELP! HELP!"

Suddenly, two more

funny little men

came running.

Wizard chased a funny little man

who chased Tubby

who chased a funny little man

who chased Snitch

who chased a funny little man

who chased Wizard.

39

"One of those men is my sister,"

Skinny shouted,

"and the girls double-crossed us."

"It was a trick," Wizard groaned.

"And we fell for it," Tubby moaned.

"It was our TRAP," Marigold snapped.

"And you fell INTO it," Gussie yelled.

"You said ONE funny little man!"

Wizard glared at Snitch.

"I only counted one,"

Snitch whined.

"Don't yell at him,"

Marigold told Wizard.

"You can't even break the code.

BUT WE CAN!"

"Yikes," Wizard yelled,

"I forgot about the code!"

"Marigold said we'd be sorry,"

Tubby reminded him.

"Marigold said we were

full of beans," Tubby told them.

"They know the code." Skinny sighed.

"Yup," Wizard said.

"If we let them join our club,

they will tell us the code.

We will *have* to let them

join our club."

"We will let you join our club."

Wizard smiled.

"Let us WHAT?" Marigold demanded.

"Join our club," Tubby said.

"Your WHAT?" Gussie shouted.

"CLUB," Snitch screamed.

"Wait," Skinny yelled,

"I have broken the code!

I can read the letter!"

Skinny held the side of the paper
with the writing toward the light.
Now he was looking at
the other side of the paper.
"It's written backward," he said,
and he read it out loud.

48

"Hold everything," Wizard shouted,

"we know the code,

so we don't need you!"

"Need us where?" Marigold asked.

"In our club," Wizard told her.

"We don't want to join
your dumb old club," Marigold said.

"You don't want to WHAT?"
Wizard shouted.

"Join your dumb old club,"

Gussie called out.

"Our WHAT?" Tubby demanded.

"Dumb old club," Rosie yelled.

"You stepped on my thumb,"

Rosie said.

"You're dumb," Gussie said.

"Anyway,

we are starting our own club,"

Marigold said.

"A club of their own!"

Wizard groaned.

"With their tricks,

and their traps," Tubby said.

"And their code," Skinny said.

"And their beards!" Snitch added.

"We *are* full of beans," Tubby said.

"Okay, okay!"

Wizard gave up.

"We will give them

another chance."

"You don't need your own club,"

Skinny said. "Join ours."

"NO!"

"You could use our clubhouse,"

Snitch told Marigold.

"NO!"

"I will share my cookies," Tubby said.

"NO!"

Wizard didn't say a word.

Wizard listened.

Then Wizard yelled,

"Okay! Okay!

We will take down the sign

that says NO GIRLS."

"Now you're talking," Marigold said.

"What shall we call our club?"
she asked.
"What's the matter with
Wizard, Private Eye?"
asked Wizard.

"Plenty," Marigold snapped.

"Wizard and Company?"

"Try again, Wizard,"
Marigold told him.

"How about Wizard and Girls?"
Snitch cried.

"I know," Skinny said. "Let's put
Wizard and Marigold together
and call ourselves The Wizmars."

"Now THAT'S fair," Marigold agreed.

"Shake," said Wizard.

And they did.

The Beginning